The Day
The Birds
Came Calling

Fulton Books, Inc.
Meadville, PA

Published by Fulton Books 2021

ISBN 978-1-64952-941-1 (hardcover)
ISBN 978-1-64952-942-8 (digital)

Printed in the United States of America

The Day The Birds Came Calling

Linda Roberts-Betsch

Kiki, age eight, was walking down the front hall stairs of her house. It was a sunny and bright March day. A wreath made of twigs, berries, and small leaves was hanging outside on the glass front door. As she looked through the door's windowpane, her eyes caught a flutter of something. She wondered what it was but paid no attention.

The next day, Kiki came down the same stairs. Partway down, she saw the flutter again. She stopped to look. She kept *very* still. Then she saw it—a small gray-brown bird with its wings all aflutter. The little bird was looking at the door wreath with interest. Kiki wondered what the little bird was doing, but she had to eat her breakfast and get to school.

When Kiki came home from school that day, she went to the front door to see if the little bird was there. She saw not one, but *two* birds fluttering around the wreath on the door. Maybe they wanted to look inside the house. Kiki thought that would be very unusual…because wild birds don't get near people. Kiki had not told her brother, Kip, age six, or her parents about the birds. It was her secret.

For the next two days, when Kiki got out of bed, she ran down the steps to see if the birds were still there. The birds were fluttering around again. They were so cute that she started calling them "my birds." On the second day, when she looked out again, she saw what seemed to be a bird's nest hidden deep inside the twig wreath. She said out loud to herself, "Oh wow! My birds have built a nest." The nest was the same color as the wreath, so it was not easily seen. She no longer had to wonder what the birds had been doing. Mystery solved—her birds had built a nest where the mother bird could lay her eggs.

Kiki could no longer keep this a secret. She just *had* to tell her family. Since she was Kip's big sister, she knew he should learn about the birds too! Kip was *so happy* to hear about the birds' nest. For the next few days, the entire family watched the nest. They were careful to not get too close or bother the birds. The two birds were often seen "tweeting" to each other. Soon, Kiki and Kip asked their mother to use her binoculars to watch the nest more closely. The mother bird was seen sitting and sitting and sitting on the nest. The daddy bird would come visit often and would sometimes sit on the nest too.

One day after school, Kiki and Kip saw that the bird was not sitting on the nest. With the binoculars, the two were so *excited* to see *five tiny eggs* in the nest. Every day before and after school, they watched the nest. They watched… and watched…and watched. They told their parents they could not wait to see what would happen. Their parents started watching more too. The family also had three small dogs who lived in the house. The family talked more about how to avoid disturbing the birds and the nest.

Do not disturb
bird's nest

The three dogs and the family had to get used to going out the back door instead of the front door. Kiki and Kip taped a sign to the front door that said, "Do Not Disturb Bird Nest."

The family watched the nest for another twelve days while one bird would sit on the nest and the other bird would visit to bring food. *Then guess what happened?* On day 13, the family saw that one of the birds was putting something in the nest. They could see the *very tiny baby birds* with *very* fuzzy hair. *The eggs had hatched!* Kiki and Kip could see that these *very tiny* baby birds with *very* fuzzy hair would open their *tiny* beaks to be fed small tiny pieces of worms, insects, and seeds by their bird family. Kiki and Kip told their school classes about the baby birds, and their teachers said they were now called "hatchlings" since they were no longer in the eggs.

The family had so much fun watching the mother bird sit on the nest and feed the hatchlings every day. Daddy bird still came by often to visit or sit in the nest too. Kiki and Kip were so happy to see the babies get bigger and bigger. Sometimes they saw their little fuzzy heads moving back and forth in the nest. The schoolteachers now called them "nestlings" because they were too young to leave the nest.

Then one day, when Kiki and Kip came down the stairs to see the birds before going to school, they could not find them. They were all gone even though the nest was still there. When they told their parents, their mother said that she would look at her cellphone that could show a view of the front porch from their doorbell camera. They all looked at the cellphone video of the porch. They saw that in the early morning hours, when no one in the house was up, and it was still dark, all these little birds were flying all around the porch. Then...*they all flew away!*

At school that morning, when the classes heard the news, the teachers said they were now called "fledglings" because they had fled the nest. When Kiki and Kip came home from school that day, their mother helped them take down the wreath from the front door. They carefully took the nest out of the wreath to save it. The family was sad to see the bird family move out, but they were so happy the fledglings had learned to fly away…as birds were meant to do.

Kiki and Kip took turns taking the nest to school to show their school friends. Kiki said she really missed "my birds." She was proud that as Kip's big sister; she had helped him learn about the birds too. Now the dogs started going back out the front door again. The seasons changed to summer, fall, winter, and back to spring again.

One spring day, Kip was walking down the front hall steps. He noticed this little bird fluttering around the wreath on the front door. He ran to tell Kiki. Can you guess what happened next? Yes, the same birds were back to build a nest again.

And that was THE DAY THE BIRDS CAME CALLING.

21

22

About the Author

Linda Roberts-Betsch lives in Alpharetta, Georgia, with her husband, Jeff. They are parents to two sons and seven grandchildren. This is Linda's first children's book. She has published many scholarly articles as a result of her education and career. Linda earned degrees in nursing (BSN) and child development/family relations (MSHE) from East Carolina University. She also earned a master's degree in nursing (MSN, maternal-child health) and a doctor of science degree (DSN) from the University of Alabama/Birmingham. Linda has had an extensive academic career in nursing education and university administration. She currently holds the title of Professor of nursing and vice president for academic affairs emerita as awarded by the University System of Georgia in 2011. Linda has served on the board of directors for several non-profit community organizations involving literacy, leadership, and the arts. Her hobbies include reading, traveling, and musical theater.

CPSIA information can be obtained
at www.ICGtesting.com
Printed in the USA
LVHW070855180821
695422LV00021B/230